DISNEY · PIXAR

TOY STORY 2

MOVIE THEATRE

Storybook & Movie Projector®

adapted by Cynthia Stierle
illustrated by Disney Storybook Artists

Reader's
Digest
Children's Books®

Pleasantville, New York • Montréal, Québec • Bath, United Kingdom

Disney · PIXAR

TOY STORY 2

Woody and Buzz were both toys, and they belonged to a boy named Andy. Woody was an old-fashioned cowboy doll. Buzz Lightyear was a space ranger toy.

It was a big day in Andy's room. Andy was going to Cowboy Camp, and he was taking Woody with him. Andy ran into his room.

There was just enough time to play with his two favorite toys one last time. But as he played with Woody and Buzz, Andy didn't realize that Woody's sleeve was caught in Buzz's arm. When he tried to pull Woody and Buzz apart, Woody's arm began to tear! Now Woody was in no shape to go anywhere with Andy.

After Andy had left, Buzz discovered that Andy's mom had decided to have a yard sale. She took Wheezy, an old penguin, for the sale. But Woody couldn't let Wheezy be sold!

At the yard sale, Woody found Wheezy in a box, and pulled him out. Wheezy was safe. But Woody fell to the ground. Then a man named Al saw him.

Al owned a toy store and knew Woody was a valuable toy. Al tried to hide Woody in a pile of other yard-sale stuff, but Andy's mom refused to sell Woody. As the toys in Andy's room watched from the window, Al stole Woody, stuffed him into his bag, and quickly left.

Buzz wasn't about to let his best friend get stolen. As Al drove away, Buzz raced after him. Buzz grabbed the bumper of Al's car, but he couldn't hang on. As he fell, he noted the car's license plate, LZTYBRN.

 Al took Woody back to his apartment. Then he put on a chicken suit and left to make a TV commercial for the toy store. At Al's Toy Barn, you could get all the toys you could buy for a "buck, buck, buck."

While Al was gone, Woody looked around. Al had all kinds of things with Woody's picture on them. Everywhere Woody looked, he saw himself!

A frisky toy horse raced up and took Woody for a ride. A cowgirl doll grabbed Woody and gave him a big hug. "Yee-hah!" she cried. "It's you! It's really you!"

Woody didn't know what she was talking about until she showed him an old TV show called *Woody's Roundup*. He learned that he was the star of the show! The other characters were Bullseye the horse, Jessie the cowgirl, and the Prospector. Al had a Prospector doll, too.

The Prospector was thrilled to meet Woody. "We've waited a long time for this day," he said.

Disk 2
1

Back in Andy's room, the toys worked
on a plan to rescue Woody. Buzz typed
the license plate letters into Mr. Spell.
"LZTYBRN," said Mr. Spell, "Al's Toy
Barn!" Quickly, they turned on the TV.
When the commercial for the store came
on, Etch A Sketch copied the map with
directions. Then Slinky Dog carefully
lowered Buzz and Rex out the window and
down to the ground.

Meanwhile, when Al came home, he
grabbed Woody off the shelf. But as he did,
Woody's torn arm fell off!

Al was horrified because was planning to sell Woody and all the Roundup gang to a museum in Japan. He couldn't sell the toys as a set without Woody!

But Andy's toys were getting closer. Hiding under traffic cones, they crossed a busy street to get to Al's Toy Barn. Inside, they searched the aisles for Woody.

Woody wasn't there. They soon realized he must be trapped in Al's apartment!

Luckily, Al came into the store a short time later. The toys sneaked into his bag as he was leaving.

When the toys finally got to Al's apartment, they tried to rescue Woody. Slinky Dog even trapped Jesse and Bullseye in his coils!

"These are my new friends," Woody said. Then he explained to Buzz and the other toys that he had decided to stay with the Roundup gang.

Woody felt bad. He knew he belonged to Andy—it even said so on the bottom of his boot. Woody realized Andy needed him. He turned to the Roundup gang and asked them to come to Andy's house with him.

Disk 3

Jessie and Bullseye were excited, but the Prospector tried to stop him. He had never been out of his box, and he liked it that way. And he really wanted to go to Japan! He knew he could get into the museum only if they all went.

Then Al came home. He packed all the Roundup toys into a case, and got into the elevator. He was going to the airport to catch a flight to Japan! Slinky Dog stretched down the elevator shaft and tried to free Woody. He was almost there but the Prospector popped up, and yanked Woody back down again. The Prospector was determined to get on that plane to Japan!

Woody's friends were not about to give up on Woody. Luckily, they found an empty Pizza Planet truck idling nearby. They followed Al to the airport. Once again, it was Andy's toys to the rescue! At the airport, the toys tracked down Al's suitcase. Buzz opened the case and POW—the Prospector jumped out and punched Buzz. "No one does that to my friend!" Woody yelled, tackling the Prospector.

Buzz, Slinky Dog, and Rex were able to rescue Woody and Bullseye, but Jessie was still trapped in the suitcase that was headed to the plane! Woody was determined to save her, and he raced after the suitcase.

Just as the plane was about to take off, Woody freed Jessie. They were dangling dangerously from the plane's cargo hold when Buzz rode up on Bullseye.